Scholastic's

The Magic School Bus ®

GETS A BRIGHT IDEA

A Book About Light

SCHOLASTIC INC.

New York   Toronto   London   Auckland   Sydney   Mexico City   New Delhi   Hong Kong

From an episode of the animated TV series
produced by Scholastic Productions, Inc.
Based on *The Magic School Bus* books
written by Joanna Cole and illustrated by Bruce Degen.

TV tie-in adaptation by Nancy White and illustrated by John Speirs.
TV script written by Ronnie Krauss.

ISBN 0-439-10274-X

12 11 10 9 8 7 6 5 4 3 2 1   9/9 0 1 2 3 4/0

Printed in the U.S.A.
First Scholastic printing, November 1999

"Amazing! Awesome!" That's what the kids in my class were saying about the terrific Light Show. The theater was filled with kids from all the schools in town. Even Arnold's cousin Janet was there, but she was in a bad mood.

"This show is so boring," Janet said. "A yawnburger with a side of snores. We should have gone to a magic show instead."

At least a magic show would have a few surprises.

In the lobby after the show, Janet said, "What a snooze! I could do better than that — I could do something *magic* with light." Then she looked scared, and a little sneaky. "But I can't right now because of the ghost in the theater!"

Keesha laughed. "Good one, Janet. But there are no ghosts."

"Now you've done it," Janet said. "You've made the ghost really angry. If anything bad happens to us, it's your fault."

Just then the lights went out!

Even though we all *knew* ghosts weren't real, we ran as fast as we could out of the theater. Luckily for us, our teacher, Ms. Frizzle, was coming around the corner in a stretch limo. The limo looked a lot like our school bus. (But why would that surprise you?)

Ms. Frizzle stepped out of the limo. The Friz wears some pretty amazing outfits, but this one was really dazzling! When she asked if everyone was here and ready to go, we looked around. Janet and Arnold were missing!

We all went back into the theater to look for Janet and Arnold.
It was dark and spooky in the theater lobby.

"Light needs a source, of course," Ms. Frizzle explained. "It has to come from somewhere."

Then she turned on her earrings!

That's why we're really glad that we have Ms. Frizzle for a teacher. Not every teacher has earrings that light up.

We followed Ms. Frizzle's earrings into the main part of the theater. "Your earrings are great," Keesha said to Ms. Frizzle. "But we need more light to find Arnold and Janet. This theater is humongous!"

This is when things started getting really weird.

We were standing on the stage. Everything around us was dark. And then . . . for just a second . . . we saw a huge ghostly image of Arnold. We could see right through him, and then he just disappeared! Arnold looked so spooky, but Keesha was certain that it was just Janet playing a trick on us.

"We'll never find Arnold and Janet unless we get some light in here," Keesha said. "Can't you do something, Ms. Frizzle?"

"At your service, Keesha," said the Friz. "Hit it, Liz."

All of a sudden, the stage floor started to rise. As we went up on a platform, the bus rose out of a giant trapdoor.

Not only did our bus have a giant lightbulb on top . . . it also had some kind of huge funnel sticking out of it. "Time to shed some light on this ghost story," the Friz said, pointing to the funnel.

"Do you, by any chance, want us to go in there?" Keesha asked.

"Well, if you want to brighten up the night, you have to be light!" Ms. Frizzle answered.

Keesha jumped into the funnel and turned into light! She came shooting out of the bus-bulb straight toward the Friz.

When Ms. Frizzle caught her, Keesha was Keesha again.

"I'm going, all right—straight dooooown!"

"Can we be light, too?" asked Wanda.

"Dazzle me," called Ms. Frizzle from down below.

"I'll take that as a yes," said Wanda.

Everyone jumped into the light funnel. Even though we all started at the same source, we shot straight out in different directions and ended up all over the place. As soon as we landed somewhere, we turned back into ourselves.

"If I hadn't hit this wall, I would have kept right on going!"

Carlos sped across the theater and grabbed onto a rope attached to a pulley. His weight pulled down on the rope . . . and the rope pulled up a backdrop with a cemetery scene painted on it. Then Ralphie smashed right into the backdrop!

"I get it!" Keesha cried. "Light travels in straight lines away from its source until it runs into something."

D.A. and Tim had landed at the side of the stage.

D.A. found a flashlight. But when she turned it on, they got a big scare!

WH...WH...WHAT'S THAT?

The spooky hand Tim saw on the wall turned out to be only the shadow of a cardboard tree.

"Because light travels in straight lines and can't go around things, the light from my flashlight hits the tree but never makes it to the wall," D.A. said. "That's how a shadow is made."

Meanwhile, we were still trying to figure out how to find Arnold and Janet. "We need to find a way to aim the light so we can see what's going on up there," Keesha said, pointing to a dark corner.

"How about this?" Ms. Frizzle said. She brought out a large mirror and turned it at an angle. "Show them how it's done, Liz!" she called.

Liz jumped into the light funnel, then streaked out toward the mirror. She hit the mirror, bounced off it, and zipped right up to the dark corner! For an instant the corner was lit up. Then Liz hit the wall and turned back into herself.

"That's great," Carlos said. "But the light from the bus-bulb is going out in all directions. How do we get it to go up to that corner?"

"We need something like this thing," Keesha said, holding up an odd-looking light. "This will shine the light in one direction."

"That's an old-fashioned footlight," Ms. Frizzle explained. "It was used to light the floor of the stage before there were electric lights. And I think there should be something on the bus that looks just like that — only bigger, of course."

We ran over to the bus-bulb. "I think I see a footlight attachment!" Carlos called. He pulled on it, and the footlight popped right up! The giant footlight caused the light to shine in one direction instead of spreading out all around the bulb.

We aimed the bus-bulb upward, and we could see Arnold's "ghost" again, bigger and brighter than ever!

But Ralphie had an interesting question. "Aren't ghosts supposed to disappear when you shine a light at them? How come this 'ghost' just gets clearer?"

"That's what happens to real things when you shine a light on them," Keesha said. That really made us think. Maybe this wasn't a real ghost.

To find the light, follow the light.

The light proves it! This IS a trick.

Next thing we knew, Keesha was climbing back into the light funnel.

She shot all the way backstage and smashed smack into Arnold's "ghost" — except it wasn't a ghost at all. It was a pane of glass hanging from two wires, and Keesha bounced right off it!

Yee-haaaaaaa!

Ping!

After Keesha bounced off the glass, she grabbed a rope that was hanging from the ceiling. When she looked around, she saw how Janet made Arnold's ghost.

I was right! It wasn't Arnold's ghost . . . it was Arnold's reflection!

Keesha and the rest of us figured out how Janet's trick works. Janet shines a light on Arnold . . . the light bounces off him, then bounces *again* off the piece of glass . . . and then down to where we are. And because Janet uses glass instead of a mirror, we can see Arnold's reflection *and* what's behind the glass. That's why we could see through him— like a ghost!

A minute later, Keesha came running up onto the stage, yelling, "GHOOOOST!"

We didn't know what was going on. When she got close to us she whispered, "Pretend to be scared. I'm playing a trick on Janet."

"We've got to get out of here fast!" Keesha yelled. We knew it was part of the act, but we all started yelling. We headed for the street.

Meanwhile, backstage in the theater, Janet was talking to Arnold. Arnold still hadn't figured out that Janet was playing a trick on everyone. "The coast is clear," Janet told Arnold. "It's safe to go."

Just then the bus-bulb light went out. Carlos sneaked back into the theater, put his hand over Arnold's mouth, and pulled him away, leaving Janet all alone in the dark.

Janet looked up and saw a scary ghost floating near the balcony. The "ghost" was really Keesha's image bouncing off the glass! Now Janet was getting a taste of her own trick!

Janet was really scared. She ran out of the theater as if she'd seen a ghost!

Out on the street, Janet saw Keesha's ghost outfit. "You tricked me!" she yelled.

"You tricked us first, Janet, so we tricked you back," Keesha said. "But thanks to you, we figured out how light really works."

"Does this mean you think I'm *brighter* than all of you?" asked Janet.

"Let's put it this way," Ms. Frizzle said. "With you around, there's never a dull moment!"

Ask the Editor

Telephone: Ring! Ring!

Editor: Magic School Bus here, Editor speaking.

Kid Caller: I just read your book on light and—

Editor: And you're calling to tell me it was *brilliant*, right?

Kid Caller: Well, er . . . yeah. But I've never seen a streak of light travel from place to place the way we saw the kids move when they were lights.

Editor: You're right! Light travels so fast that you can't tell that it takes any time at all for it to move from place to place.

Kid Caller: So you slowed the kids way down when they became light so we could watch what it does and how it moves?

Editor: You got it!

Kids seem to be getting brighter and brighter these days!

Pepper's Ghost

Janet's trick is an old magician's trick called Pepper's Ghost. You and a grown-up friend can do it together. Here's how:

1. Take a cardboard box and paint the inside black.

2. Cut a medium-sized window in one side of the box.

3. Make a cardboard window frame, stretch some plastic wrap across it, and fit it in the box on a slant. (You might have to tape it in place.)

4. Make a cardboard cutout of whatever you want to be your ghost object, and put it on the floor of the box.

5. Close up the box.

6. Cut a hole in the top of the box so a flashlight can shine on your "ghost" object without lighting up the back of the box.

7. Turn on the flashlight, and you'll see a reflection of your object in the plastic, making a "ghost" appear in the window.

8. Turn off the light, and your "ghost" disappears because there's no light to create the reflection!